A is for Adam

Marc Richard

DEDICATION

For my Crew: Laura Cantwell, Rhonda Corson, Marshall Clowers, Juliana Conforto, Johannes Debler, Tony Dodds, Michelle Dupree, Alfred Gaeta, Lisa Hicks, Mike Ikirt, Chris Karluk, Marcel Langlois, Alan Leveson, Larry Marek, Norma Miles, Nate Olsen, Caleb Orion, Nick Perry, John Questore, Martha Reed, Robert Rock, Shelley Simons, Jason Smith, Joseph Souza,Cathy Stanley, Laura Stuteville, Dawn Taylor, Virna Thibault, Jill Thibodeau, Shanna Tidwell and Justin Tyler. Thank you for making this possible.

Contents

1. The Sixth Day

 bug crawled across his face, waking him up.

"All right, all right. I'm up. Jesus." He wasn't sure who Jesus was, since he was the only living human in the Universe; it just seemed like the right thing to say. The bug crawled across his face every morning around this time, so he never overslept. He wasn't sure what would happen if he did, since he didn't have a job. He rolled over to check the alarm clock by his nightstand. But there was no alarm clock. Or nightstand. Or time.

The bug was hungry. Adam found a large bright green leaf, picked it up off the ground, blew off the dirt that had accumulated on it, and set it in front of his bug friend. Why the insect couldn't find his own damned food was beyond him. But his was not to question the ways of the Universe.

He went to a corner of the room where he slept in his hut and went to a tall thing, called a bureau, made from mud and leaves. He had cleverly added things called "drawers" that slid in and out to hide and protect the delicate leaves he used to make the clothes. And to feed the bug. He opened the top one. The drawer was full of the same leaf, but for variety and style, each leaf was slightly different. Each leaf had a vine, tied in a large loop, pushed through it There was really no need for clothing, since modesty was a thing of the future. No, this wasn't out of modesty at all. This was totally utilitarian, to keep the sheep from nobbling at his privates. He had made several hundred versions of these leaf clothes, mostly out of boredom. On the last few he had made, he figured out how to make the knot adjustable in case he gained or lost weight. There were plenty of animals for him to slaughter, so he never had to go hungry. But it was a giant pain to hunt, kill, prepare, then cook an animal, every single day. So, some days he went without eating and lost a little weight. Fruits and vegetables were abundant, but they did very little to keep the weight on. Plus, he was getting sick of the lack of variety.

One food he was curious about was the Fruit that hung from the special tree in the center of the garden. He was very tempted to eat one, just to see what it tasted like, since it looked delicious. But God said no. He was never sure why God said no. Something about how the tree possessed knowledge, and if he ate the fruits that blossomed from it, he would suddenly know things. At first it all sounded a little like science fiction to him, and a lot like bullshit. And, so what if he knew these so-called "forbidden" things? What was the harm in that? But who was he to question God? Soon, however, he began to think maybe there really was some truth to this "knowledge-thing." He often caught one goat eating a Fruit that had fallen from the Tree, and he was starting to believe that the goat was becoming smarter than him. It had even learned how to walk on its hind legs and had even begun speaking Arabic. This seemed a little too close to evolution, and it quite surprised him that God didn't put a stop to that right away. If this kept up, soon the monkeys may turn into people. And that was some really messed up stuff. He stared at the Tree. Some day he would eat one of those Fruits. He'd be damned if he was going to be outwitted by a goat.

He stood at the edge of his garden, watering it. And a very large garden it was. Although large compared to what, he wasn't sure. There were fig trees and pear trees, juniper bushes and blueberry bushes. He would have been proud of it, were pride not a sin. It was beautiful, and he took great pains to make it that way. If any visitors showed up, it would greet them with the most amazing sights and intoxicating smells. He had enough to feed an army, and it was a shame to let this all be for nothing. He couldn't help but feel that it was all wasteful. No matter; it wasn't he that was wasting it. It was whoever created this garden. Was it sinful to think things like that? He hoped not. So far, he was without sin, and he wished to keep it that way.

He had never been far enough out into the garden to lose sight of his own hut, so he did not understand just how massive it was. He had plenty to eat all around him, and there was no need to venture out any farther. But he was sure there was more to see out there. More delights and wonderments that he hadn't discovered yet. So, why not? He was curious and bored. He was hoping curiosity and boredom weren't sins. He couldn't wait until God came out with a list. Or handbook. Or something.

2. The Belladonna Chronicles

e left behind the figs and junipers and little prepackaged bags of cashews. Farther and farther in he went, till soon he lost sight of his hut. He hoped he didn't get lost, but then again, home was where you hung your fig leaf, so he could set up shop anywhere he liked, really.

Such sights were there to greet him! Strange green objects and yellow ones and brown ones. Things he had never seen before, not even in his craziest dreams. Why hadn't he ventured out before today? He could have been eating all these delicious-looking things. He strolled around, naming things as he went, because that was his privilege, seeing he was the only human in existence. He called this one kiwi and that one coconut, this one clam and that one olive, this one cucumber and that one Doug. On and on he strolled through the garden, tasting a little of this, a little of that. Some things were perfect right off the vine, like the things he now called grapes. Other things he needed to cook, such as the large, orange object he decided for some cute reason to call pumpkin. Due to his naivety, it never occurred to him that some things were not edible, and were just there for him to admire only with his eyes, such as nice, innocent-looking fruit that resembled what he called a blueberry. He decided to name this belladonna, after the lead singer of Anthrax. Hmm. They tasted decent, perhaps a little too sweet. He picked them one by one off the vine, shoving them into his mouth as he did so. It briefly entered his mind that maybe he should save room for other treats he felt sure he would find as he continued his explorations. But the more he ate of these, the better they tasted. He felt like a glutton. He wasn't sure what a glutton was, but he pictured one in his mind. It resembled a beaver, with larger teeth and a piss-poor attitude. It scampered around the belladonna shrub, looking to take a bite out of one of Adam's bare feet. He kicked the creature. It sprouted wings in midair, then flew away to better things. The berries jumped off the bush and shot into his mouth, burning with the heat of a thousand suns. The ground opened up beneath him, threatening to swallow him whole. Cthulu's many tentacles shot up from the earth, wrapping around him. He felt comforted by the sweet caresses, as Cthulu lifted him higher and higher into the stratosphere. He wondered who in the world this Cthulu was. When he realized he didn't know, the tentacles holding him fast suddenly went bye-bye. He felt himself dropping from thousands of feet in the air. The ground was approaching fast, and he briefly got a glimpse of his future face looking like a plate of corned beef hash. Suddenly, he remembered the parachute he had on his back, fashioned out of pterodactyl skin. He pulled the ripcord. It occurred to him at that moment that he had inadvertently packed the beak in the deployment bag instead of the skin. Faster and faster he plummeted towards the earth. As he approached inevitable demise, structures began rising out of the ground, shooting straight skyward. His beak-a-chute caught on the antenna of one structure, but not before the cord had wrapped around his neck. Now he hung there, thousands of feet in the air, strangling. A giant monkey, seeing his dilemma, began climbing the structure. He made it quickly to the top and began punching airplanes out of the sky. *Never mind the airplanes, save me!* He thought but could not say, as he was choking to death. The monkey grabbed the cord and untangled it from the antenna. He climbed back down the structure, with Adam in one hand, and set him gently on the ground. Adam sat stunned, wondering what would happen next, but the monkey just turned and stomped away. *Wait, monkey! How can I repay you?* But with just a few strides, the monkey was already in the next zip code. A massive explosion suddenly rocked the ground, and structures all started crashing down around him. The apocalypse happened much sooner than he had expected. *Oh well,* he thought, *at least I have all these books to read.* But he stumbled, and his glasses fell off his face. But wait! He didn't wear glasses. What the hell were glasses? Glass had not been invented yet, but he *did* have a pair of spectacles he fashioned out of plastic cups. He had 15/20 vision, but no other people in existence also meant no scales, vision or otherwise. All he knew was that when he put those plastic cups up to his eyes, he saw better. Especially when he put a little water in them, as a refractor.

That's the last thought he had before he collapsed in the garden, fast asleep.

3. Eve

e awoke hours later, wrapped warmly in a kangaroo pelt blanket, and a recently deceased bunny under his head as a pillow. He should have been comfortable, for this was his preferred way of sleeping; however, he was not. Something didn't feel right. For one, he was way out in the middle of the garden, probably lost. Who covered him up? This also didn't feel like his usual bunny, since he'd had his bunny pillow for a long time, and he'd broken it in exactly the way he liked it. This bunny seemed too new. Too stiff, which made his head cock at a strange angle, giving him a crick in his neck.

Another thing bothering him was an annoying pain in his side. He reached down, touching where the sensation and pain was.

This didn't feel right at all. Flinging aside the pelt, he got a good look at his body. What the heck? A huge gash in his side was dripping blood onto the dirt. *Kidney thieves!* He thought and plunged his hand inside the opening. Everything seemed fine, pretty much. His heart was still there. His lungs were still there, although he could have figured that out without feeling them, since he was breathing. He reached all the way around, straining his elbow as he did so, and felt for his kidneys. One, two. Both there. Well, that sure was a relief. Although he knew he could have lived with just one kidney, he preferred having both of them, in case something came up. Pulling his arm back, his hand noticed something on the way out. Or rather, the lack of something. He was missing a rib. There it was, the portion where it was broken off, sticking out like a snapped tree limb.

"Hey, would you mind giving me back the covers?" asked a sweet-sounding voice. "I'm freezing over here."

Someone was lying right next to him. How did he not notice that before? Probably the whole gash-pain-thing was making it hard to pay attention to anything else. This was the first person he'd ever met, besides himself.

"Steve?" Adam asked

"Eve," the person answered.

"Ha-ha! Hurrah! Praise Yahweh! Our Creator has finally given me a companion!" He suddenly looked remorseful. "Sorry, I have had no time to clean the place up. I wasn't expecting company."

"That's all right," Eve responded. "I mean, the world is a rather large place for just one person to keep tidy."

His eyes fell to her chest. "Yes, I suppose it is," he said, distractedly.

"Umm, can I help you?" Eve asked.

"Please, excuse my eyes. They have their own mind."

"Quite all r..."

"What are those???" he asked excitedly.

"Those are boobies. They are our Creator's gift to you."

"Do they hurt?"

"No, not really. They just add a little weight to my front side, is all. Does that hurt?" she asked, pointing to his thing he had yet to name. He thought of calling it a *glumph*, but he wasn't sure. Sometimes, especially when it got a little too cold, it felt like a *plink*.

"No, does yours?" he asked, looking down at his midsection. "Oh, pardon me. Where is my fig leaf?"

She pointed to her own crotch area. "I borrowed yours. Sorry for not asking, but I thought you were dead. You weren't responding, and you were bleeding heavily."

"No problem. I have several of them back at the house. And I wasn't dead; I was only what I call completely wasted. Do yourself a favor and stay away from those things that look like blueberries, because they aren't blueberries.

"I don't even know what blueberries are, so it'll be hard for me to stay away from the things that look like them but aren't them."

"Don't worry, I'll show you around. Now, you still haven't answered my question."

"Which was?" she asked.

"Does your glumph hurt?"

"I don't have one," she answered, turning six shades of red.

"What do you mean, you don't have one?" he asked.

She moved the fig leaf aside a little, so he could see what was down there. He'd seen those before on other animals. He'd often thought of putting his thing in them, after watching some animals do it. But it embarrassed him, as he felt he didn't measure up.

But here was one he may get into, after some persuasion and perhaps a few cups of fermented grape juice.

"I'm sorry, are you disappointed?" she asked.

"Oh no. No, not at all," he said, turning a few shades of red. "I like the fact that you have one of those. I call them squash blossoms."

"That's kind of cute," she said, rolling her eyes.

"Say, what do I call you, anyway?" he asked.

"As I have said, you can call me Eve," she said.

"Yes, but what are you, one-who-is-almost-like-me-yet- different?"

"I am called woman. Meaning from man. The Creator took your rib and used it to make me."

"What?" he asked.

"Yeah, sounds kind of like witchery to me. But who are we to question? Anyhow, I have come from you, and am not original, therefore I will always be less than you and subservient to you. If I ever begin acting autonomous or start speaking my mind, it is imperative you strike me down with a switch, but no larger than your thumb." She looked down at his crotch again. "Or your glumph."

"Sounds like a sweet deal," he answered.

"It is," she answered. "Enjoy it while you can. In thousands of years, this arrangement will change."

"Yeah, I doubt it."

4. Tiptoe Through the Garden

o, Riblet, here's the Garden," said Adam. "I think it's pretty nice. Bountiful bounties and plentiful plenties, and all that."

"It's Eve," Eve insisted. "Please don't call me Riblet."

"But it's cute," Adam said. "Just like you."

"Flattery will get you nowhere with me. Just remember, Eve. Not Riblet. I don't call you Dirt."

"Hey, hey, now. I'm very sensitive about that. So, I'm made of dirt. So what? You can call me Clay, if you like. That sounds more like a name to me. But please don't call me Dirt. In fact," he said, "Adam would be preferable. What are you doing?"

Eve was carving words in the sand with a stick.

ADAM + EVE 4EVA

"Seriously?" he asked. "Already with the sappy stuff?"

She grabbed him painfully by the upper arm, her nails digging into his flesh. "Listen, you little twerp. I don't like this anymore than you do. There I was, floating around in the Ether, and suddenly God yanks a rib out of some schmuck and use it to turn me into his companion. Someone to keep him company for all eternity. That's my sole job. I'll never be a doctor or a lawyer or an executive at a big corporation with a nice big office on the top floor with a view. I'll just be a side-kick. I'm lucky I even got a name. Believe me, first opportunity I get to burrow my way out of your life, I'm taking it. Till then, It's AD-AM + EVE 4EVA. Get it?"

"Wow, I'm sorry. Here." Adam handed her a slice of pumpkin, which she chewed for a brief second, then spat out. "Bleccch. That's horrible. What are you trying to do, poison me?"

"Poison you? My only companion till the end of time? No way. I just kind of wanted a second opinion on this lousy fruit."

"Well, it's terrible."

"Agreed. But look what I did." He pointed over to another pumpkin sitting in the garden, minding its own business. A crude face was carved into it.

"I don't get it," she said.

"What's not to get? It's art."

"What's art?" she asked.

"A concept I invented. It's where you create something out of something else."

"That's blasphemy." Eve scolded. "Only God can create something out of something else."

"Well, obviously that's not true," he said. "I mean, just look at this face." He pointed to the pumpkin again. "And anyway, God created something out of nothing, like the Universe, but it was something useful. Art is really not useful at all. "

"So, if it's not useful, why do it?"

"It's meant to make people happy. Or sad. Or just evoke any kind of emotion at all. Maybe, in that way, it is useful."

"Well, I think it's dumb."

"I think it'll catch on," said Adam.

"Catch on with whom?" she asked.

"I don't know. Maybe there will be other people someday. I have ribs to spare. Anyway,

I think art is cool. Especially this, um, Jack-o-'lantern."

"Jack-o-'lantern?"

"Yeah, I think it sounds Irish, don't you?"

"What's Irish?" she asked.

"Never mind."

"Personally, I think it's a waste of food," said Eve.

"So?" he answered. "What else are we going to do with it? Besides, is wasting food really all that bad?"

"I'm not sure," she said. "I guess I don't know the difference between good and bad."

"Yes," he said. "If only there was a way to know the difference between good and bad..."

"Yes," she said. "If only."

"Look, things here aren't so terrible. Plenty of delicious things to eat, pumpkin aside, lots of privacy, I mean, lots of privacy, and just look around you."

She did.

"Breathtaking, huh?"

"I guess I could do worse. It is nice."

"This is all ours. To do with as we please. Look, I know it was probably cool being formless floating around in the Ether, but you're here now. Let's make the best of it. Come on, what do you say? ADAM + EVE

4...?"

"Eva," she said, somewhat bashfully. Maybe it wouldn't be so bad here in the long run.

5. Another Day for You and Me in Paradise

hey entered the warm confines of the hut.

"Come on, who's in the mood for some delicious grub?" Adam asked.

Eve looked off in the distance in silence.

"I said, who's in the mood for some delicious grub?"

Eve's head swiveled. "Oh, were you talking to me just now?"

"Who else would I be talking to?" Asked Adam.

"Precisely," she said. "I'm the only other one here. Therefore, your question is stupid."

"Is this what I have to look forward to?" Adam muttered to himself.

"What was that?" Asked Eve.

"I said, who's in the mood for some delicious grub?"

Eve sighed. "Fine. Me. I am."

"All righty, then. Give me time to prepare. Take some time. Explore the grounds."

"You cook?" she asked.

"Yes, I do. And I'm a good cook, if I say so myself. Although soon this will change, as you'll be doing all the cooking, dusting cobwebs, vacuuming dirt, and ironing my fig leaves with a hot rock. What do you think about that? Sweet deal, huh?"

"Can I go back to being a rib?" asked Eve.

"What? And deny me the precious gift our Lord has given to me? No, thank you. I'd much rather be short a rib. Besides, you know what they say guys can do once they have ribs removed?"

"Enlighten me," Eve said.

"Well, umm... I uh... Well, I have you now, so I guess I don't have to worry about it."

"Ha. We'll see about that."

"Aww, well, I think once you try my cooking, you'll think differently," said Adam.

Eve gave Adam a look for the first time. It wasn't a look he liked at all. And it was one that all men would come to learn they needed to fear.

"Uh, anyway, why don't you go for a walk? It's a beautiful day today. Go climb some trees, hit a rock with a stick, eat some fruit."

"Yeah, I think it may do me some good to get some alone time."

"Already?" Adam said. "It hasn't even been a whole day."

"Well, you know. Give it time." And with that, she left the hut.

She made her way back through the garden, sampling this and that. One thing she found out is that there were certain things that she loved. And certain things she detested. For instance, the thing that Adam called banana (which Adam confessed that when he ran out of ideas, he just started throwing letters together) was delicious. The thing that Adam called onion, well, that was terrible.

"Adam?" she shouted, and he poked his head out of the window.

"Yes, dear?"

"That onion is just terrible. Awful. Who in the world would ever eat such a thing?"

"Ah, yes. True, the onion is wretched," Adam said, then added: "But wait till you try it cooked. It completely changes."

"I'll take your word for it," she muttered.

A few more steps later, and there, in front

of her, was the Tree. It didn't look very magical. It looked like any of the others, except for the Fruit hanging from it. Though even the Fruit didn't look extraordinary to her, other than the fact that this was the only tree that had grown them. Based strictly on looks, it was nothing she felt she just had to eat. What was intriguing, however, was the fact that God told Adam not to eat from the Tree. The strange powers this Fruit had, bestowing on the consumer a great knowledge, particularly the ultimate knowledge of Good and Evil, that was something that made it hard to resist. Why was that such a bad thing? And why would God place the Tree there with the sole purpose of not eating from it? Temptation? It made no sense. Was God a trickster?

"Did I hear ssssomeone ssssay that they wanted to know of Good and Evil?" hissed a voice from the tree.

"Did I say that?" she asked.

"Yessss, you did," the voice said.

"I don't remember saying that," she said.

"Well, you did."

"Hmph. Show yourself, creature."

A long, green slithery thing made its way out around the branch so she could get a good look at it.

"Adam!" she shouted.

His head poked out of the window again. "I'm trying to make a pie," he shouted back. "What is it now?"

"Why is this garden hose talking to me?" she asked.

"That's not a garden hose. It's a snake."

"Then why is this snake talking to me?"

"I think he's Satan," Adam yelled.

"Oh, well, that makes sense. Get thee behind me, Satan," she spoke. And with that, the snake disappeared from the tree and crept up from behind her onto her shoulders.

"Aaah! Don't sneak up on someone like that!" she yelled.

"Ssssorry, but you ssssaid..."

"I know what I said. It's a figure of speech."

"Oh. And anyway, I'm not Sssatan," he whispered in her ear. "I'm just a sssnake."

"Nuh-uh. No way. You... you're Evil!" she said to him.

"How would you know, if you haven't eaten the Fruit that givessss you that knowledge?"

He had a point. It was a classic Catch-22. For all she knew, the snake could be Good, and biting into the fruit could be a good

29

thing. But until she bit the fruit, she wouldn't know.

Suddenly, the goat came walking by on its hind legs. This was the goat that had eaten of the Fruit. This was the goat that could walk upright, talk, and sing. This was the goat that Adam had named Phil Collins.

"I can feel it comin' in the air tonight," he sang.

"Oh, Lord," she said. "What should I do? It's just a fruit. Why all the fuss? And look at what it did for the goat."

"Yessss," the snake hissed. "Look at what it did for the goat."

A fog rolled quickly in. Soon, all that was visible was the Tree, the Fruit, and the snake. What should she do? This was the land of confusion. Should she? Shouldn't she? Tree. Fruit. Snake. The only thing missing was God. The answer seemed obvious.

She took a bite. The fog rolled away.

"How issss it?" the snake asked.

"Meh. It's all right, I guess," she said, and tossed the rest of the Fruit into a nearby bush where it promptly caught fire.

"You'll regret this," came a voice from the bush.

"I guess?" she answered. "Honestly, I don't

see what all the fuss was about. I don't feel any smarter yet. Calculus still eludes me. I'd eat more of this Fruit if I could learn calculus, or even physics. Take what I did the other day, for example. I dropped a pumpkin and a pea from the roof, and they hit the ground at the same time. That still makes no sense to me! Will I learn the answers to that?

"... Hello? Anything?"

The bush did not speak. No reply at all.

6. That's a Lot of Trouble for a Pie

vening had approached fast. The hut would have been enshrouded in darkness, had it not been for the little fiery pillars everywhere. She wasn't sure what they were, but they were trés romantic.

Adam looked at Eve. "Huh? Not bad, right?"

"It'll do," she understated.

"It'll do?"

"Just kidding. It's gorgeous."

"Well, you're my lady. And I wanna treat you right. Remember, God said I could beat you whenever you get out of line, but He also said to cherish you. Which I find a contradictory statement, but there you have it. I'm sure

God won't make a habit of contradicting Himself."

"No," Eve agreed. "I'm sure He won't."

"Here, have some fermented juniper berries."

He poured a little in her Solo cup and she took a sip. The first spit-take in history drenched his face in gin, which was now mixed with Eve's saliva.

"No good?" he asked.

"No good? It's atrocious."

"Yeah, I think so too. But it can get you pretty hammered. That's why I keep it around."

"Typical male," she said.

"What the hell is that supposed to mean?"

"Not sure," she replied. "Anyway, do you have any of that fermented grape juice?"

"Wine?" he asked.

"Dooo youuu haave anny fermented graaape juiice?" she whined.

"No, I call it... ah, never mind. Here." He poured her a cup.

She sipped it. "Much better. So, tell me, dear. What are these little tapered things on fire, and where did you find them?"

"Those are candles. And I found them at the quaintest dollar store."

"Really?" she asked.

"No, you ninny. I made them. From beeswax."

"What's beeswax?"

"Well, see, there are these things called bees that have built themselves a fine little home in the back garden. I haven't figured out the use of these creatures yet. I tried eating a dead one, and it didn't really taste much like anything. I don't think it has much nutritional value. However, they secrete the most amazing stuff that tastes wonderful in baking, or even made into a drink and fermented."

"Do you ferment everything?" she asked.

"Oh, believe me," he said, with a wink. "I have tried."

"So, what about the wax?" she asked. And was soon sorry she did.

"Well, they vomit honey from their stomachs, and they secrete clear, tasteless, brittle wax flakes from the abdomen glands. The bees then chew and mold them, making a series of hexagons. It takes thousands of flakes to make one gram of wax. (Source: Wikipedia). Each candle I made is about a hundred grams. I guess if I could count that's about 50 candles. Can you imagine how many flakes that took? To use the wax, I put a chunk into a pot, then put that on top of the thing I call a stove and melt it, pour in a mold, and put what I call a wick in it. That is where you put a flame and what you see burning. I make the wicks from hemp and sheep nut veins."

She looked at him from the corner of her eye.

"Yeah. It's exactly what it sounds like," clarified Adam. "Anyway, let's eat."

He walked over to the area of the hut he called the kitchen, grabbed some meat off what he called the stove, and slapped down two pieces. One for Eve, and one for himself, onto paper plates. When he was building his hut, he had used mud, leaves, twigs, and branches. He had made one room to sleep, and a room called a kitchen. He was thinking about a room to use the bathroom because he really was tired of always having to go poop in front of all the animals. He had made a thing he called a stove and oven. He had dug a circular hole in the ground and lined it with rocks. He got the idea after realizing long after the sun went down, the rocks he had to sit on would always stay hot for hours. Then on the side of the hole, he stacked a circle of rocks and kept it filled with twigs, branches, leaves, and kindling. Sometimes the smoke was thick, so he luckily had the foresight to leave a hole in the roof above the stove and when it rained, he could not cook.

"What are these things you just put the meat on?" she asked.

"Those are paper plates. I made those too, by chopping down a tree and cutting the wood into chips, then I chemically separated the cellulose fibers into a pulp, pressed it and rolled it into a shape I call paper, then cut them into these shapes you see here called plates.

"Sounds like a lot of work," she said.

"Yes, but they save me from having to wash dishes."

He then scooped the side dishes onto the plates.

Eve ate ravenously. Although she'd sampled a few things from the garden, this was the first actual meal she'd had. And it was delicious.

"Wow," she said. "This is amazing. What are we eating?"

"Venison steak come from deer. This from one I hunted, skinned, and butchered, then tossed two of what I call steaks in a pan. I add a little butter, garlic, and rosemary for flavor. Then I made some whipped potatoes with this cool thing I call a whisk. I made it with the bones of little dead birds and used hair from a horse's tail to tie them together at one end. They are very thin and small and make the potatoes fluffy, but your arm gets exhausted when you use it. And you have to go fast. Now that I think about it, I use that arm for something very similar but... Oh, UHM, never mind. Back to the food. Then I dug up these things I call carrots and sautéed them in sage and brown butter."

"Marvelous."

"It's nothing, really. Anyone can cook if they get bored enough. I've had plenty of time to experiment, believe me."

"Which begs the question," said Eve. "How long have you been here?"

"I really don't know. A while. Time is such a relative thing, isn't it? Like, how do I even mark the passage of time when nothing really changes? I mean, do I count the number of times the Sun has gone around the Earth? Do I use this here watch?"

Adam pointed to his wrist, and the black band wrapped around it. On the top was a digital display.

"Where did that come from?" Asked Eve.

"I don't have the foggiest. I'm not even sure

what it does. I assume the numbers supposedly measure or mark time somehow, but I'm not sure what each number means. Bah, no bother. I'll figure it out at some point, I guess."

Before she knew it, she had finished eating her dinner.

"Now, who's ready for dessert?" Adam asked.

"No!" she shouted. "I want to live in the Garden with you. Please, don't banish me to live in the desert! I've done nothing wrong!"

"Not desert," Adam said. "Dessert. It's delicious and wonderful and it makes you feel... well, the opposite of how the desert would make you feel." He raced back to the kitchen and brought back a dish that was exuding the most intoxicating aroma. "Here. This is dessert."

"Sorry. I think it will take me a while to get used to the words you came up with to name things."

"It's all right. Perhaps I could have called this something else. The words *do* sound very similar. I suppose I could have called it pudding, like the British, but then what would I call actual pudding? Tell you what. I'll let you name this dish."

"Really?" she asked.

"Sure. Why not?"

"Terrific! I think I will name this... pie."

"Yeah, okay. And that's the last time I will let you name something."

"Why? I think pie is a cute word."

"Let me tell you a story. Out in the garden grows this tall, unassuming-looking grass that I call wheat. When the stalks start getting heavy, I know it's time to harvest. I separate each kernel from the stalk. I make sure there is no dirt or foreign materials left in the batch, and then I soak them to soften them up. Then I break up each kernel and separate what I call endosperm, for lack of a better term, from what I call bran. The bran makes me poop too much, but the animals seem to like it. The other stuff I turn into what I call flour. I then mix the flower with salt that I gathered from the mines a few miles away, the sugar that I harvested from the cane, and butter which comes from a whole other process I'd rather not talk about. Then I roll it out into a sheet, fit it into this dish, and fill the middle with pears, raisins, cherries, and any other fruits that in season, as well as more sugar, this tree bark which I call cinnamon, and other spices that I have either plucked from a tree or bush, or from the ground. I bake it in an oven for quite some time, depending on how hot the fire is, trying to control the flame enough to cook thoroughly without burning it, and cut it with a hand-carved stone knife, and you wanna call it pie?"

"No good?"

7. Confession

heir first-time making love was a strange jumble of tangled limbs, awkward fumbling, trying to find where things go, and a lot of messiness, and although we could have predicted all of that nonsense, Adam and Eve thought it would have gone much smoother. After all, God had created them with puzzle-piece parts, and it shouldn't have been that odd a trick to put them together. Once they got going, however, it was pure magic. It went on for quite some time, pushing, pulling, thrusting, retreating, over and over again, and just when they were beginning to tire of all the nonsense, they both got the nice surprise at the end that makes rainbows and fireworks appear from out of nowhere.

Lying in bed in post-coital bliss. Eve felt a

little delirious from all the spinning that had just happened, and her mouth was running before her brain caught up. Women always have to ruin it by talking after. Adam, as we could have guessed, was sound asleep, snoring away. This began a long tradition of men doing the same thing for ages. Still, to this day, we call it the Sleep of Adam. Huh? We don't? Well, then I am taking credit for coining the phrase. Yes, you heard it here first, folks. So, if anyone ever refers to a man's heavy sleep at the end of sex as the Sleep of Adam, remember, that's me.

"Adam?" she said.

Snore.

"Adam?" she said.

Snore.

"Adam??" she said, with a nudge of her elbow.

"Ngungg" he muttered.

"I have to say I underestimated you. Tonight. The candles. The most wonderful dinner. Making love. It was so romantic. You are so loving, so passionate, so caring. You know what I mean?"

"Nggrrrg," he muttered.

Sigh. "That's why I feel like I have to tell you something. I can't keep it a secret. We're partners, and partners share everything, right?"

"Ngrargh," he muttered.

"Well, I guess they do. I mean, we're the only partners I know. Human, anyway. But I've watched the animals, the ones who are monogamous, and they seem to share everything. So, I suppose we should too, right?"

"Nrrrff," he muttered.

Sigh again. "All right, here goes. I ate the Forbidden Fruit."

"You what???" Adam's body sprang bolt upright in bed. A look entered his eyes that Eve couldn't distinguish between fear or anger. Perhaps it was both.

"I ate the Forbidden Fruit. Sorry..." she said, apprehensively.

He cradled his head in both hands. "Sorry. Sorry? My God, do you know what you've done?"

"Not really. It was just a bite. Nothing more than a nibble, really."

"It doesn't matter. God explicitly told us not to eat of the Fruit. Oh man, we're in deep doo-doo."

"Well, technically he told *you*. He said nothing to me about it."

"Have you forgotten that you are me, Riblet?"

"Only by a technicality. I'm an individual person, too."

"Obviously not, since you can't even make proper decisions for yourself."

"Sorry..."

"Sorry. Sorry."

"Yes, Adam. I'm very sorry. I don't know what else to say."

"Well, you better think of something," said Adam.

"We don't even know what this means. Maybe nothing will happen."

"This could be the end of the world as we know it."

"I feel fine," she said. "Nothing's changed. I don't feel any smarter, or like I know anything I didn't before. Some Tree of Knowledge. What is he doing testing us with Fruit, anyway? He knows all there is to do in this life is to eat, sleep, and crap. Eventually, we would end up eating the Fruit. Why would he put it there? To tempt us? It makes no sense."

Adam glared.

"So, I have failed a test. Big deal. I'm sure this will just be one of many tests we'll fail in our lifetime. We're allowed mistakes." She looked at Adam. After a brief pause, she asked, "Aren't we?"

He shook his head. "I don't know. I don't think so."

"Well, that's insane. I mean, we're only human."

"What is that supposed to mean?"

"I don't know. I just think it is part of the human condition. We're given free will and can do as we choose. Therefore, it only goes to follow that we will make some mistakes."

"This," Adam said, "was not a mistake. This was disobedience, plain and simple. We will be in so much trouble. Go to sleep. We'll talk about this in the morning."

It was difficult for Adam to get back to sleep, knowing all the punishments that God possibly had in store for them, but the Sleep of Adam (I really think that's a winner) soon overcame him, and he was out.

Some time passed, but not enough to suit Adam. He wanted to sleep, not listen to her. Yes, that would have been ideal. But no, Eve had to run her yapper again.

"Adam?"

"Ngerrrrgh!"

"I just had a thought. It would be a much nicer life if I could let myself live in the now a little more. Then I realized that everything we see travels at the speed of light and is not instantaneous. Therefore, everything we think we're experiencing now is actually in the past. Cool, huh? Or is that depressing? Maybe this Fruit *is* working.

"Phlrrrp."

"Adam?"

"Mmmmm?"

"Tomorrow, will you go out to the garden with me, and take a bite of Fruit? I mean, we have nothing to lose at this point. I already messed things up. I just think we should do everything together. Isn't that what couples do, do everything together? I mean, I don't know what behavior God expects from humans, but I noticed that sheep and goats do everything together. Will you, please, take a bite of the Fruit for me? Please?"

"Oh my God, woman!" Adam blasphemed. "Fine! I will take a bite. Now for the love of God, will you please let me get some sleep?"

"Sure," Eve giggled. "Goodnight."

"You mean good morning." Adam looked at the digital numbers on his watch. "I think."

8. Eden's End

hey stood there, hand in hand, at the foot of the Tree. The core she had tossed on the ground had long since vanished, most likely eaten by that very intelligent goat.

"I'm nervous," Adam said.

"Don't be. Like I said, I already ate the Fruit. Whatever damaged I have caused, I can't undo. You may as well grab one and take a bite and get it over with."

"But what if I'm *not* in trouble? I mean, it's you that took the bite, innit? Maybe you'll be the one punished, and I'll be okay. My record's clean. I mean, it'll suck to lose you, but I have more ribs, so..."

A slap landed across his face. "How dare you!" she shouted.

"No good?"

"No. No good. As you said, we are one. What happens to me happens to you. And how can you even think about loving another rib?"

"Yes, dear. I'm sorry, dear," he said, plucking a Fruit from the Tree.

Phil Collins the goat walks by once again. "I can feel it coming in the air tonight," he sang again.

"Oh Lord," Eve said. "He sang that before."

"Yeah, he likes that song," said Adam. "Especially at ominous times like these."

STOP! A voice came from above.

"Say wha?" Adam asked.

DO NOT, I REPEAT, DO NOT, EAT OF THIS FRUIT!

Adam and Eve looked at each other. "God," they both said.

"Listen, God," began Adam. "I appreciate everything you've done for me. Really. I do. But what's the deal with this Tree? Why would you put it here just to tempt us? Seems kind of cruel, dunnit?"

I AM THE GOD OF THE OLD TESTAMENT. AND I AM CRUEL! (I'll tone it down a bit when Jesus arrives.) NOW, DO AS I SAY! (Although, it is your choice.)

"So, can you please answer me what the

deal is with this Tree?"

THIS IS THE TREE OF KNOWLEDGE. IF YOU EAT OF THE FRUIT YOU'LL...KNOW THINGS.

"Oh yeah? Like what things?" Adam asked, although he already knew the answer.

LIKE GOOD AND EVIL. YOU'LL KNOW IF THE THINGS YOU DO ARE BAD OR GOOD!

"Forgive me for asking, dear Lord, but don't we want to know those things? Don't you want us to do good?"

YES! YOU BETTER BE GOOD, FOR GOODNESS SAKE! BUT I DON'T WANT YOU TO KNOW THAT THE THING YOU'RE DOING IS GOOD UNTIL I TELL YOU THAT IT'S GOOD, AND ONLY THEN CAN I...OH, TO HELL WITH IT. I'M GOD! DON'T QUESTION MY METHODS! YOU KNOW, THE WHOLE MYSTERIOUS WAYS AND ALL THAT.

"Then why did the snake ask me to eat the Fruit?" Eve asked.

I'M SORRY, IS SHE TALKING?

"Rude," said Eve.

"Then why did the snake ask her to eat the Fruit?" Adam repeated.

I SENT THE SNAKE FROM THE

DARKNESS. IT WAS EVIL PERSONIFIED... SNAKE-IFIED.

"Aha!" Eve said. "How was I supposed to know that if I hadn't eaten the Fruit?"

YEAH, CAN WE GET AN INTERPRETER HERE?

"Hey! Rude!" said Eve again.

"How was she supposed to know the snake was evil if she hadn't eaten the Fruit? Don't you see? It's a Catch-22!"

JOSEPH HELLER. GOOD BOOK. ALTHOUGH I DON'T QUITE CARE FOR THE NAME OF THE AUTHOR. LISTEN, I HAVE STUFF TO DO, LIKE REST. DO WHAT YOU WANT. YOU HAVE FREE WILL. GOOD-BYE.

"So, did he really mean we should do what we want?" asked Adam.

"Just take a bite.," said Eve.

Adam took a rather large bite.

"You know," he said, with his mouth full of food, "maybe we're not the only intelligent species out there."

"Didn't I tell you? Instant brains!" said Eve.

"Hmm. Maybe you shouldn't eat any more of this Fruit. We don't want you becoming too smart. After all, what good is an intelligent woman?"

"Ugh. Men are pigs!" she shouted, storming off.

"Kidding!" he shouted back at her, tossing the half-eaten Fruit.

Adam stood there watching, mouth agape, as the Fruit struck the ground with the force of a meteorite, smashing through the surface of the planet and creating a sucking vacuum that pulled Adam and Eve down through and out of the Garden of Eden forever.

9. Gifts from Heaven

dam awoke to find himself in the middle of a desolate landscape. His head was pounding. Eve lay on his left, as still as the air around him.

"Eve?" he said. No response.

"Eve??" he said, a little more urgently. Still nothing.

He put his ear up to her mouth. No breath. She was dead. At least, he thought that's what that meant. He rolled her over onto her back. If she wouldn't breathe, then he would shove his breath into her mouth hole until she had enough that she could do it on her own. He forced all the air in his own lungs into hers. Nothing. He did it again. Nothing. One more time. Her chest remained still. Perhaps if he pressed up and down on her chest, maybe then it would start moving. He did it once, twice, three times. Stayin' alive...stayin' alive. The phrase was repeating over and over in his head rhythmically. He breathed into her mouth again, compressed her chest again, alternating back and forth until, success! Her open eyes focused on Adam and she smiled.

"Eve! You're alive! See, God? You're not the only one who can do it. I gave her life, too!"

Her smile turned to worry as she got a look at the desert all around her. "Where are we?" she asked.

"I don't know. But this definitely isn't Eden anymore."

Incidentally, they were in Mesopotamia, otherwise known as Iraq. Oddly enough, it wasn't much different from modern-day Iraq.

"I told you I didn't want to live in the desert!" she shouted. "Bring me back to the Garden!"

"I didn't do this, Eve."

"Why? Why did you bring us here?"

"You gotta believe me, sweetie. I didn't bring us here. I don't understand where we are, or how we got here."

"We're gonna die!" she yelles. "We're gonna die out here in the desert!"

Adam grabbed he by the shoulders. "Eve,

listen to me. Calm down. You gotta keep your wits. Strange things happen all the time in my life. I'm used to it by now. Everything is a new experience. This is just another new experience. I'll get through this like I've gotten through everything. We'll get through this. We'll find our way back, I'm sure of it. And if not, we must make the best of this."

"Easy for you to say," said Eve.

"Maybe. Life has been easy so far. Why should I expect any different going forward? You know dear, this could be the start of something WATCH OUT!"

Adam shoved her out of the way, barely avoiding getting hit by a large colorful object falling from the sky. It hit the ground with a loud Whumph!

"What in the world is that?" asked Eve.

"Looks like some type of gift."

It was. A gift, standing about four feet tall, wrapped in snowman wrapping paper, all done up with a large red bow.

"Who's it from?" she asked. "There's no tag on it."

"Hmm. Oh, wait. There's a card."

"Open it, open it!!" she said a little too enthusiastically, given their situation.

"All right, I'm getting to it."

Inside the envelope was a very tasteful card. On the front was a picture of a fat man in a sleigh being pulled through the air by eight caribou. Happy Holidays it said, written in glittery font. He opened it up. "May Your Days Be Merry and Bright!" it said on the inside. A little too generic, if you ask me. Handwritten on the opposite page was a note. It was from you-know-who.

"He even writes in all caps," Adam said. "Jeesh."

DEAR ADAM AND EVE,

YOU HAVE DISOBEYED ME FOR THE FIRST AND LAST TIME. I GAVE YOU FREE WILL, SO I GUESS A LITTLE OF THIS IS ON MY SHOULDERS. HOWEVER, YOU NEED TO KNOW THAT YOUR ACTIONS HAVE CONSEQUENCES. I'M SORRY IF THIS IS A VERY HARSH PUNISHMENT, BUT AS YOU KNOW, I AM A VERY CRUEL AND UNFORGIVING GOD. FOR NOW. IN THOUSANDS OF YEARS I MAY LIGHTEN UP A LITTLE. SINCE YOU NOW KNOW THE DIFFERENCE BETWEEN GOOD AND EVIL, IT IS MY DUTY TO INFORM YOU THAT YOU HAVE DISOBEYED ME AND SINNED BY

EATING OF THE FRUIT. YOUR PUNISHMENTS WILL BE MANY AND GREAT.

YOU ARE TO LIVE IN THE DESERT. NO MORE WILL YOU BE ABLE TO VISIT THE GARDEN THAT I SO LOVINGLY CREATED FOR YOU. IT HAS NOW BEEN DEMOLISHED TO MAKE WAY FOR LUXURY CONDOS.

ADAM, YOU WILL NO LONGER BE PROVIDED WITH FREE FOOD. YOU WILL NOW TILL THE LAND AND GROW VEGETATION BY YOURSELF. I HAVE LEFT YOU YOUR GOAT, SO YOU MAY EAT OF ITS FLESH IF YOU WISH AND GET MILK, ALTHOUGH IT WILL BE DIFFICULT TO DO, SINCE PHIL COLLINS IS A MALE GOAT. WHATEVER MILK YOU DO SQUEEZE FROM HIM IS PROBABLY NOT MILK, SO I WOULDN'T DRINK IT IF I WERE YOU.

EVE, YOUR LOVE-MAKING SESSION FROM THE OTHER NIGHT HAS PRODUCED A CHILD INSIDE OF YOUR BODY. IN THE WEEKS TO COME, YOU WILL KNOW THE HORRIBLE PAIN THAT IS CHILDBIRTH.

YOU ARE NO LONGER PURE. YOU

NOW KNOW OF THE DIFFERENCE BE-
TWEEN GOOD AND EVIL, AND YOU
WILL BE FOREVER LABELED AS SIN-
NERS. AS FURTHER CONSEQUENCE,
EVERY CHILD BORN AFTERWARD WILL
HAVE SIN BORN INTO THEM. YOUR
CHILDREN WILL BE RIGHT LITTLE BAS-
TARDS, THEY WILL. GOOD LUCK WITH
THEM.

INSIDE THE PACKAGE IS THE
AFOREMENTIONED GOAT, SOME GAR-
DENING EQUIPMENT, AS WELL AS A
VARIETY OF SEEDS TO PRODUCE NU-
MEROUS FRUITS AND VEGETABLES.
I LEFT YOU PLENTY OF FORBIDDEN
FRUIT SEEDS, SINCE YOU SEEM TO LIKE
THEM SO MUCH.

TAKE CARE,

G.

"Hmm," Adam said. "Well, that sucks."

"Yeah," Eve agreed.

"Now look," said Adam. "I won't blame anyone, but it seriously is all your fault we're
here."

"I accept that," she said, not arguing like
Adam expected. He realized that this would
be one of the few times in history that this
would happen, so he figured he'd better not

push it by elaborating on just how badly she screwed them both.

"I'm sorry. Really, I am. Listen, let's go see if we can find a spot to make shelter and we'll figure out what we should do from there, okay?"

He dried her tears with his hand as she nodded.

"Hold on a minute, Eve. You have something in your ear."

"Baaah, get it out get it out!!" she screamed.

"Okay, I will, just calm down. Look, it's a twig. Huh. You must have gotten tangled in the bush before your fault. Fault? Did I say your fault? I meant your fall. Haha. Hey, good thing you didn't land in the burning bush. You would probably still be on fire right now."

"What Was up with that bush, anyway? Always burning, never burnt. That's not how chemistry is supposed to work." Tears came in a river down her cheeks.

"Aww, what's wrong?" he asked.

"You know," she said, after her tears dried up and she could finally speak, "Im gonna miss the weirdness. Nothing there made sense, but it was home, you know? Now we get this...this...this...nowhere to live in. This plain, boring nowhere."

"Meh. It may be nowhere, but I would say it's anything but boring. Presents falling from the sky. We still have Phil Collins, the talking goat. I have a feeling things could be interesting around here. And don't think of it as a desert. Think of it as a beach. Now, don't just stand there. Help me unwrap this package."

10. Seeds

hey unwrapped the gift together. Beneath the snowman wrapping paper was a plain cardboard box. Although neither of them had seen cardboard before, Adm was already turning ideas over in his head about how he could make it. He was pretty sure that it wasn't much different from the paper plates he had made.

"Well," Adam said as he looked over at Eve, "Here goes."

God hadn't bothered taping the box, which was just as well, because Adam probably would have been more occupied with the novelty of the tape than what was inside the box. God had instead, folded flap over flap, in the Escher-style that we all know how to do when there is no tape. This was convenient for God, but not so convenient for Adam, as he was now fully occupied with the novelty of the fold.

"Look at this, Eve. Look at how God folded the flaps. It's like a never-ending staircase."

"Yeah, I'm not really sure what that is." As the world had yet to become crowded, and the concept of family had yet to be invented, there was never any need to build any other levels, hence, no staircases.

Adam, who had dreamed of staircases, tried to explain. "Staircase, you know...Uh, like a ladder, kinda, but...umm...different. Kinda."

"Sure," Eve said. "Well, let's open this." She put her hand under one flap, and Adam stopped her. "Wait. Just take a second and look at this. Don't you see? You follow the flaps to the left, they go up, up, up forever. Follow them to the right and they go forever down. I bet if I found a perfectly round rock and put it on one of the flaps, it would just go to the right, down forever. This is incredible. Only God could create something like this."

"Yeah, no. Look," said Eve, as she unfolded the flaps and refolded them, over and over.

Adam's eyes widened. "That's magic!" he said. "Witch!"

Eve laughed. "No, I'm not a witch, dude. If you look closely, you'll notice that the flaps all rise slightly even though it looks like..."

"Yep. Okay," Interrupted Adam. "Hey, let's see what's inside!"

Inside the box was another box. And inside that one, another box.

"Ahh, God," said Adam. "Ever the trickster. Good one."

The third box had been partially chewed through.

"Phil Collins!" Adam shouted excitedly.

"About damn time," Phil Collins said. "I thought you guys were going to stand there chit-chatting all day. Thought I would starve to death in there; I was about to eat all these seeds."

"Yeah, let's see what we got," said Eve.

"Wow, look at all this," said Adam. "We got a diggy-thing, a little claw-thing, a thing with a pointy-thing on it. Another flat-thing with a wobbly-thing. A thing with a thing under it. And, ooh, look at this thing. Ooh, we got seeds, look at all the seeds we got. Lemmesee, we got pumpkin seeds, pear seeds, tomato seeds, wow there must be hundreds of different varieties of seeds here. God hooked us up. See? He doesn't hate us. We have it made here."

"This is a joke. Don't you get it? We have all these seeds to plant, and nowhere to plant them. Just miles and miles of sand. Plants need water. Where is the water? How the hell is anything going to grow in this? God hooked us up? No, God set us up. We're going to die out here, Adam. We'll starve to death."

"Nah, we'll be all right," Adam said.

"I don't know how you can be so positive right now."

"Because being negative is a waste of time. It's not productive at all. And it's not realistic. Things have a way of working themselves out for me. Always. I was feeling lonely, you appeared one day. I was tiring of the boring selection of fruits and vegetables, God showed me the way to other delicious ones. He provides."

Eve laughed. So hard. "You idiot."

"What?"

"God doesn't provide. He doesn't watch out for us. Not anymore. God abandoned us. He's gone. This box was his parting gift. There is no more God."

"That makes no sense, Eve. You can't get rid of God. He is there all the time. Like our breath and our heartbeat."

"Which will also leave us, at some point."

"Oh, Eve. So full of negativity."

"Really?" Eve asked. "Really, Adam? We really should save this for when we got hungry, but here. You need it." She kicked the sand away from a fallen Forbidden Fruit that had gotten sucked down into the abyss with them.

"I'm not really..."

"Eat. It has nothing to do with hunger. You need to see for yourself."

"Well, okay," said Adam.

And the more he ate, the more the dumb optimistic expression left his face. The Fruit was allowing the understanding to seep its way into his brain.

"You see?" she asked. "You getting it now?"

"No," said Adam, "no, no, no. It can't be. Eve? God is dead, isn't he?"

"Yeah. He is. To us, anyway. This is it, Adam. It's just you and me and Phil Collins until we die of starvation in this awful place."

"Phil? Say it ain't so, Phil!" Adam pleaded.

Phil shook his head. "Listen. You know I love you, but I just can't take this," he said, and walked away.

"Phil, come back!" Adam shouted.

And Phil would come back. Even though he was a thousand times smarter than Adam, he still needed time to process all of this.

11. Sometimes You Gotta Make Do

ife in the desert turned out to be not so bad after all. Their home wasn't anything that would appear in any magazines, for sure, but it was cozy, and protected them from the blazing sun. They had to travel far for water, and even when they found little pools here and there, they were usually tiny. They had to use the water for drinking only, for Adam, Eve, and Phil Collins. So, the water that glued the sand together to make the mud for their hut wasn't actually water, but the byproduct of water that happens after it flows through the digestive system. Stink? A little. But after the sun had baked all the impurities out of the urine-coated sand, the smell was no longer there, and they were left with a very sturdy hut that stood up fairly well against the hot desert winds.

Growing produce had been a bit of a struggle, and at times Adam got to thinking maybe he should change what he named produce to nonproduce. It didn't have that much of a ring to it, however, so he kept the old term and hoped for the best.

Digging through the sand hadn't been much of a challenge; it was finding the right spots to dig in. They needed to be damp spots, which, as I have said, were few and far between. He could only plant a few seeds near each oasis he had found, for he didn't want the plants to suck up the only water there was. They needed to make sure they had enough for their own bodies to hydrate with.

It was an entire year before the first tree bore any fruit. And what a difficult year that had been. The water pools had gotten to be tens of miles away, and by the time he reached them, he had to drink half of it just to have enough strength to make it to the next one. For food, luckily the occasional desert rat would scurry by, and he would roast it over an open fire. On very rare occasions, a camel or something would get close enough so that Adam could slaughter it. By the end of the year, Adam had gotten good at hunting camels, keeping alert enough for any sign of movement despite the hallucinations being brought on from dehydration in the searing heat. Camels weren't that difficult to catch, as they weren't what you'd exactly call a fast-moving animal, but tracking them was a whole different matter. Sure, they left foot-prints in the sand, which were rare, but any time the desert breeze would blow, it would just cover them back up. The good thing is, once he had killed an animal, the meat would dry in seconds, so it would keep for quite some time. The bad news is, the meat would dry in seconds, so there was very little water content in it; far from enough for them to stay hydrated.

So, it was exactly one year later (although Adam was terrible at telling the passage of time, out here where there were no seasons made it particularly difficult) when the first Fruit blossomed on a Knowledge Tree. These were the first plants to sprout any food, so for a while, both breakfast and dinner comprised of camel-wrapped Knowledge Fruit. At first it was good. The camel meat had added a cer-tain gaminess that had been lacking in the

Fruit. After a while, they became tired of the taste, but they were always grateful that these were the first fruits to blossom. The more they ate, the smarter they became. The smarter they became, the more new and innovative ways Adam was inventing to grown more food. And so on.

Luckily, it was only a few months before other things began to produce food, and soon Adam had quite the garden growing. Although one couldn't technically call it a garden. Eden was a garden. This was more like scattered plants. But no matter. He had drawn a little map to where each plant was, and soon he knew the layout like he knew Eve's body, and didn't need a map anymore. Eve, disappointed at their love-making sessions from time to time, had wished that he had made a map of her body. But I digress. The point is, soon they were almost as comfortable there as they had been in Eden, and the beauty of it was, both Adam and Eve had made it with their own hands this time. This gave them a greater appreciation for what they had. Every time Adam looked at his surroundings (as barren as they were), his home, his gardens, everything was because of what they did. (He had quickly forgotten that God had given them the seeds and the tools to till the land in the first place, but really, who's keeping score?)

Soon they were eating like kings. Adam had invented some cool cooking devices, from the first self-cleaning oven to the first microwave. His testicles tingled every time he used it, but it cooked things in seconds. He didn't really know why he wanted things to cook so quickly, since they had nothing but time there, and often after meals they would just sit around and stare at each other with nothing to do.

All this staring led to boredom, which led to the invention of games. Tic-Tac-Toe, backgammon, pin the tail on Phil Collins. They had to get Phil wasted on wine before they played, as they used very sharp vulture bones to fasten the camel tail to his rear end. Phil had been a pretty good sport about the whole thing, oddly enough. He had forgotten, due to the wine, that he was stuck here with these yahoos for eternity.

12. Belly

old still," Eve said to Adam, and reached into his ear.

"Ow! What the..." he said, as it felt like whatever she was pulling from his ear was attached to his brain stem. Every nerve, from his neck up through his sinuses, shot up with an electric charge, and he sneezed.

"Huh. Look at this," she said, and showed him the twig she pulled from his ear.

"That's weird," replied Adam. "Remember the time when you had one in your ear?"

"No," she said.

"It was right after we had landed here from Eden."

"Don't remember."

"I'm not surprised. You were pretty dazed," said Adam. "Anyway, honey? If I say something, do you promise not to get mad?"

"No," she replied.

"No, you won't get mad, or no you won't promise to not get mad?"

"The last one."

"Okay. Never mind, then."

"Oh no," she said. "You can't do that."

"Do what?"

"You can't start something off by asking me not to get mad, then not tell me what you didn't want me to get mad about. Just spill it. I won't get mad. I promise."

"Now you're just saying that because you want me to tell you what I was going to tell you."

"Yes. I am. Now tell me."

He took a deep breath. "All right. Here goes. Now, don't take this the wrong way."

"..."

"You know, I love your body, right? I mean, your soft shoulders, your legs, your...you know."

Her eyes rolled. "Get to the point."

"It's, um, your belly. I mean, don't get me wrong. I love your belly. Love it. It's just, well, it's gotten, um, a little, um, big."

He braced himself for the punch to his jaw, but it never came. Instead, she sighed and dropped her shoulders in a melancholy fashion. "I know," she said. "I'm not sure what's going on."

"How much have you been eating?" he asked.

"You should know. We eat all of our meals together." She then added softly, "Except for the ones I sneak."

"You're sneaking meals?" he asked. "No wonder you're getting fat! Honey, you can't do that. We only have so much food to go around."

"I'm sorry. Really. I'm just always so hungry. Even right after we eat a meal, I'm still starving. It's as if I'm eating for two people."

Adam's head quickly swiveled and his eyes grew big. "Wait, what did you just say?"

"I'm sorry. Really. I'm just always so hungry. Even right after we eat a meal, I'm still starving. It's as if I'm eating for two people."

"That's it!" he shouted.

"What's it?"

"Don't you get it? You feel you're eating for two people because you are eating for two people. There's a person in there." He pointed at her stomach.

"A person?" she asked. "Are you sure?"

"Sure, I'm sure. It only makes sense."

"Yeah. It makes sense to me too. You know, once in a while I can feel it moving around in there. I thought it was terrible indigestion. But just yesterday I thought I saw an outline of a foot underneath my belly skin. Well, that's solved, I guess..." A look of fear entered her face rather quickly. "Wait, what? A person? Oh no. No! What do I do? Get it out! Get it out!"

"I can't."

"Why not?"

"What do you want me to do, rip you open?"

"Yes! If you have to," she said.

"I don't think I have to. Remember God's Christmas card, where He told you that you would have to experience the pain of childbirth?"

"Unfortunately."

"I think you will have to experience the pain of childbirth."

"Which means?"

"Which means it'll probably come out on its own."

"How?"

"I think it'll be one of two ways. It's in your stomach, right? You know how food comes out, once it's digested?"

"Oh no. No way."

"Yeah. It'll come out like poop comes out."

Adam smiled.

"What have you got to smile about?"

"Poop. Still one of my favorite words I invented. Always makes me smile."

"Adam, focus."

"All right, so anyway, yeah it may come out that way."

"Kill me now," she said.

"You'll be fine."

"Easy for you to say. Ouch, that's gonna rip me a new one."

"Heh. Yeah, probably."

"Wait, you said one of two ways. What's the other way?"

"Well, you remember how we created the baby?"

"No."

"No clue?"

"No It just started happening suddenly. One day I noticed my belly had gotten big. And before I knew it, it was moving."

"God's note said it was from our lovemaking session."

"We're never doing that again," she said.

"Haha, we'll see."

"No, I'm serious, Adam. We are never ever

doing that again."

"Baby, you know you can't resist this."

"Try me," Eve said. "So, anyway, you think it could come out of there?"

"Seems logical enough," Adam said.

"While that doesn't seem as bad, it still seems like it will hurt. Like, a lot."

"Meh," Adam said. "Nonsense. I fit in there just fine. I'm sure it will be a piece of cake."

"You fit in there just fine, all right," she agreed. "Your teeny little codpiece, anyway. Not your entire body."

"Hey, my codpiece is not teeny."

"It is when compared to a whole person!" she answered.

"Fair enough."

"Yeah."

"I don't think it'll be all that bad, you know. I mean, how big can this person be? It's small enough to fit in your stomach, right? What can it be, all of five pounds? Six at most? You'll be okay. Why, my codpiece must weigh at least four and a half."

"Dream on," she said, and with that, the conversation dropped, and soon, they forgot about the person growing inside of her for a while.

Until...

13. What Is Wrong with These Kids Today?

ain was born a little prematurely, so his birth weight was less than four pounds. However, his size was a poor predictor of his temperament, as he had the piss-poor attitude of a rhinoceros charging down a runway full of wounded peacocks. God said it would happen, and it did. Not only could the little bastard not take care of himself, he was worthless. He had no worth. He was a total waste of space. A little space, true, but a waste nonetheless. He never ate his vegetables, he ran around the house all crazy, tracking mud outdoors, vivisected defenseless animals while they were still alive, and he would always knock pictures off the wall. What a little asshole. Fuck.

Whew. I apologize for my language, but wow, what a prick.

"You know," Adam began, "I was thinking...Ow!"

"Sorry, honey. You had a really big eyebrow hair that was bugging the hell out of me."

"You couldn't have waited? I was thinking."

"Yeah, but look at this," she said, and showed him the hair she had just plucked.

"What the...?"

"Looks like a twig," she said.

"I know. Looks like the same thing we've been finding growing out of our ears lately. What do you think is going on?"

"I don't know. Must be the desert heat making out hair grow thicker or something."

"Don't you think the opposite should happen? Shouldn't our hair grow thinner instead?"

"Careful, Adam. You're treading too close to Natural Selection territory."

"Anyway, as I was saying, I was thinking. I may have a way we can get back into God's good graces and get back into Eden."

"Why? Do you not like it here? Hahaha," she said, sarcastically.

"Hahaha. As fun as this is, I want Eden back." He looked around as if someone else were listening. "I mean, I would like to get right with the Lord," he said, then whispered to Eve, "I really want Eden back."

"Okay, so what's your plan?" she asked.

"I think we should really show Him just how sorry we are. Let's jump in the river."

"Not now, Adam. Tell me what your penance idea is."

"We should jump in the river."

"Fine, but then will you tell me what your idea of penance is?"

"That's it. We get in the river."

"That's the punishment? How is that punishment?"

"We'll stay there for forty-seven days."

"Why forty-seven?" she asked.

"Why not forty-seven?"

"I would hang out in a river for a thousand days. I am so tired of this heat it'll be a welcome relief. I still don't see how that's penance."

"Don't you? We'll get all pruney."

"But where do we find a river around here?" she asked.

"That's the good news. There's one closer than we thought. The Tigris is only a couple days' trek away."

"The Tigris? Isn't that, like, icy cold?"

"It's a little chilly, yeah. But this is penance. Get it now?"

"Jeez, I guess so now. We'll die before the first hour's up."

"Maybe. But look at it this way, water problem's solved."

"Great. Where did you come up with this idea?"

"I had a vision."

"You had a vision. Well, that's nice. Did your vision include you dying of hypothermia?"

"Well...see that's the thing. I'll be in another river."

"What? Another river? Why another river?"

"It's just, I think part of our penance should be spending time away from each other. Solitude, you know? Nobody enjoys being alone. I think it'll make for lots of brownie points with the Big Guy."

"Fine, where you gonna go? Euphrates?"

"Jordan," he answered.

"Jordan?" blurted Eve. "Jordan? Are you kidding me?"

"What?" he asked.

"I suppose you're going to one of those all-inclusive resorts. Gonna lounge by the pool and drink some daiquiris?"

"What are you talking about?" asked Adam. "I'm immersing myself in the river for forty-seven days. Just like you."

"Oh, poor you. Bathing in room temperature waters while I'm freezing my butt off. That's nice."

"Listen, it's not gonna be a picnic for me either. I have to walk for weeks through the desert to get there."

Her eyebrows arched, causing a twig-hair to go schproiiinnngg!

"Well, okay. I'm hitching a ride on Phil Collins."

"You'll be sitting on Phil Collins the whole way through the desert? You'll break him! How does he feel about this?"

"I'm on my way; I'm making it," Phil sang.

"See? He's on is way. He's making it." Adam added, "That's a new song for you, Phil. Where did you learn this little ditty?"

"A little angel named Gabriel," he answered.

"See? I'll be okay. You'll be okay."

"I'll be freezing my ass off," she reminded him.

"Fine then. You know what? You only have

to stay there for forty days. How's that? I'll stay in my river for forty-seven. You stay for forty."

"What do we do about the little asshole?" Eve asked.

"Cain? Leave him. That's another side bonus. A vacation from him for a month. What do you think about that?" he asked.

"Which way's the river?" she replied.

14. Tigris

t took a couple days for Eve to make the trek across the desert to the Tigris. With every other step, she cursed Adam's name. As she sat by the bank of the icy river, dipping her toe in the water, she cursed his name loudly. Screamed it, in fact. She knew the water would be cold, but the actual feel of it on her skin brought a whole new meaning to the word.

"Oh, Adam, why did I let you talk me into this?" she asked. "Curse you, Adam! And curse your name!" she shouted into the sky, which caused a dozen birds that had been lounging along the river to fly directly up and a bright white beam of light to shine down.

"Huh?" asked Eve dumbly, as out of the bright light there appeared a beautiful figure.

An angel, most would have thought. And yes, it was an angel, but this angel had a mean streak and a penchant for mischief. Because of the knowledge she had gained from eating the Fruits, she knew right away that this was Satan himself. He approached her slowly, with gentility and grace, and placed a hand on her shoulder.

"Dear child," he said. "You don't have to do this."

"What do you mean?" asked Eve. "Of course I do."

"Why?" asked Satan. "Because Adam said so?"

"Well, yeah. I mean, I guess. He is the man of the house, after all."

"Man of the house?" Satan said. "Would a man make his woman spend forty days in freezing cold water while he lives in luxury in the golden waters of the Jordan?"

"Well, I..."

"Would a man not invite his wife to come join him in those golden waters, rather than send her away?"

"You know, I..."

"Or at the very least, would a man not come join his wife in the icy waters, rather than forcing her to endure the pain alone?"

"Hmm, you know, you have a point."

"Yes, of course I have a point. He's making you do the penance while he does nothing. It won't work. God won't forgive either of you this way. His was a dumb idea."

"Perhaps," she said. "But how do you know God won't forgive me at least?"

"Because," Satan said, with a smile, "God doesn't forgive. He banished you to here because you ate a Fruit? One that you had no idea how good or bad it was, because you hadn't eaten the Fruit yet? Does that make sense?"

"No, I suppose not."

"And get this. God told me I had to worship Adam. Not sure what that's all about. I asked God, isn't it enough to worship You, I have to worship this guy too? He's just a person and doesn't need to be worshiped."

"And what did God say?"

"He said Adam was made in His image, an extension of God himself. I then asked Him, wouldn't that be worshiping a false idol? Isn't that a sin?"

"What did God say?"

"He told me to quit arguing and get out of His face. So here I am."

"God kicked you out of Heaven?"

"Apparently."

"For how long?"

"I don't know. For good, I guess?"

"Is there nothing you can do to get back?" she asked.

"I don't know. But it sure as hell isn't standing in this cold river. God doesn't care about that. I don't wanna go back, anyway."

"Where will you go?" she asked. "You can't stay on Earth. You'll lose your angel status."

"There's a place that's far sweeter than Heaven. And it's down below."

"You mean Hell?"

"It's not as bad as everyone makes it out to be. Besides, as soon as I enter Hell's gates, the place will be that much cooler. Everyone already likes me down there." He looked at his watch. "Listen, I gotta go. Just remember what I said about Adam. He ain't shit. Look at the child he gave you. If he was so great, don't you think he could've produced something better than that Cain kid? Anyway, do what you want; it's your life. I just wouldn't get in that river if I were you. Laters."

And just as quickly as he came, he was gone.

That's it, thought Eve, I'm packing up and going home.

15. Meanwhile, on the Left Bank...

dam sat on the edge of the river in a lounge chair, daiquiri in hand. Okay, maybe he wasn't actually in the river, but he was near the river, and he took occasional dips in the water anytime he wanted to cool off a little (or do penance. Ahem). He had gathered quite the audience of animals; little birds and deer followed him around wherever he strolled. He felt like Jesus would feel in his heyday. None of this was natural; they were all instructed by God to follow him around and worship him. There wasn't one creature in the bunch that thought Adam was worth much as a human, never mind an entity that needed to be worshiped. But what could they do but follow God's orders? They really had-n't any say in the matter. If they all did what God said, perhaps they would be in a better place when they died. It never occurred to any of them they had no souls, and they weren't going anywhere.

"Get me another drink, will ya Phil?" Adam asked, and if goats had fingers, boy, Phil would sure have used one of them right then.

Phil poured him a drink from the blender, as he took another dip in the Jordan. The water was so nice! It was fantastic here; perhaps he could convince Eve to move out here with him. It sucked he had to walk all the way back to Iraq to ask her, then turn around and walk all the way back here. It was then that Adam's relaxed mind had fallen asleep, dreaming about some future time when the telephone would be invented.

Before he could drown, he was startled awake by two dolphins passing a beach ball back and forth. For a minute, they debated letting him drown, since they didn't really care much for Adam, but they needed a hu-man to throw the ball, and he would do in a pinch.

"Oh, hey Chip. Hey Dale. Thanks for stop-ping by. Here ya go," he said, and bopped the ball high in the air. Chip flicked the ball with his tail, to Dale, who caught it on his nose, and they swam away. "Bye guys!" he shouted at them.

Forty-seven days had passed of this nonsense, and it was time to head home. All he could hope was God was witnessing what a sacrifice he was making, and that he would get back into His good graces. It would certainly be a shame if he holy fuck, what was that on his shoulder? It looked like a peeling flap of skin, but it had a dry, hard, brittle consistency. It almost resembled the bark of a tree. Skin shouldn't be like that. "Ouch!" he yelped as he plucked it off. It hurt, doing that, and he watched for blood. There was no blood to follow, however, there was a clear fluid oozing from his shoulder that had the consistency of sap.

Odd, he thought. Now where was I... Oh yeah. It would be a shame if he had walked all this way and endured all this punishment for nothing. To tell you the truth, he felt a little pampered by his time at the river (No kidding!), and it would make the long, long walk back home all that more arduous.

And it was. It was arduous and strenuous and taxing, and all those other synonyms. The heat, reflected by the desert sand and thrown back up into his face, was unbearable. Thirty-foot sand serpents burrowed in and out of the dunes all around him. Giant winged creatures swooped down out of the sky and ripped away at his flesh. It briefly occurred to him that maybe this was the punishment. But then he thought, no. No, the river was the punishment. (It also briefly occurred to him he had very little concept of what punishment was.) At times he wanted to give up, but the thought of returning to Eve was enough to keep him trudging on.

At last, he arrived home. Eve was relaxing on the couch, her feet up on the ottoman. Her time must have been worse than his; she looked dead tired.

"Eve!" he exclaimed, rushing to her side to embrace her. "You made it home!"

She nodded. Pa rum-pump-pum-pum. "I did. I'm glad to see you are also back home!"

"Oh, sweetie," Adam said. "It was just terrible. The water was wet and the hot sun kept making the drinks warm, and Phil Collins could be a right prick at times. Anyway, enough about me, how was your time in the Tigris? It must have been just horrendous."

"It was all right," she said.

"All right? Care to elaborate?"

"Not really," she said. She had already made her mind up. She wouldn't tell him that she disobeyed him; it would not only make him angry, but it would surely destroy his ego. She would just let him cling to the idea that he was head of the house, and that she would do what he expected of her, if he thought it was for the greater good. She would think of it as her contribution to the wellbeing of the family.

"Fair enough," he answered. "Any word from God yet?"

"Nothing," said Eve. "Do you think we did the right thing, Adam? Do you think the punishment was enough?"

He sighed. "I don't know. I thought it was a good idea. But I assumed one of us would have heard from God right away. I was expecting visions while I was out there in the Jordan, but all I got was warm daiquiris. I have a feeling we're stuck here forever."

"Oh, I don't know," Eve said. She thought back to her chat with Satan and how God wanted him to worship Adam. "I have a feeling you're in God's good graces."

"I sure hope so," said Adam. "Now, where's my boy?" he said at too high a volume.

"Shhh. I just put him down to sleep. He's been a hellraiser all day."

"So, he survived his time alone, then?"

"Yes, he did just fine," she answered.

"Shit."

"Yeah."

A familiar face peeked around the corner. "Daddy!" Cain exclaimed and ran to his father excitedly.

"There's my boy," he said, his arms wide open for a hug from his son.

The boy ran up to his father, punched him square in the nuts, giggled, and took off.

"Come back here you little shit!" he shouted. He turned to Eve. "Did you see that? That little... I'm gonna go teach him a lesson."

"No, don't honey. He's been waiting all day for you to come home so he could do that. Just let him go back to sleep so we can get a little peace and quiet around here."

"You're right," he said. "Ugh, what do we do about him, Eve?"

"You know," she said, "I've been thinking. What do you think about having another child?"

He couldn't shake his head fast enough. "Nuh-uh. No way. No, no, no."

"Listen. Just hear me out. Maybe this next

one will turn out better. We deserve a nice child, not one that goes around cauterizing the buttholes of little bunnies. Plus," she added, "I think it would do Cain a lot of good to have a playmate. Maybe he just acts out because he's bored. I mean, we're the only other people in his world, and who wants to hang out with adults all the time? Come on, what do you say? Let's have another baby."

And so, Abel was born unto the world. They called him Abel because they were hoping he would have a little more aptitude than his brother when he was born. Alas, it was not true. He was born a blubbering mass of tissue just like his brother. Although he was a lot more pleasant to be around, he was miles behind his brother in terms of overall brain capacity. He was a simple boy who'd never vivisect a desert rat like Cain, because he was gentle, yes, but also because he had no clue how to vivisect anything. In fact, he didn't know what vivisect meant. In fact, he did not words over two syllables.

16. Eve's Restless Night

nd so, time went on. The pipe dream that Eve had about Cain calming down and acting like a decent person once he had a brother was far-fetched. In fact, Cain became much worse. The special needs that Abel required demanded much of Adam and Eve's attention, plus, let's face it, they loved him more. So, Cain was more than a little jealous.

Although Cain hated Abel with every ounce of his being, having his brother around encouraged his creativity, as he continually invented new ways to torture him. He had enjoyed the time he tortured him by covering him with honey to attract fire ants and then left him out in the desert sun. And the time he had tied him up in the basement. Which he himself had to dig, just to have a basement for to tie him up in the first place. And removing him from his 'Friends and Family' plan without notice. Cain was a cruel boy.

One night, Eve awoke, startled from a most horrible dream. "Adam? Adam, wake up."

"Hmmm."

"Adam, I have to tell you about the most horrible dream I had."

"Blrgr."

"Yes, yes. Later. But first you must listen while I tell you about my dream."

"Blrgr?"

"Oh, all right," Eve said, and performed her oral duties. It wasn't clear to her why she did this, since it in no way gave her any pleasure. Also, it yielded no children. Perhaps this was why Adam liked it so much. Maybe he and Eve were through having kids. She couldn't possibly blame him, after watching the shit-show that was Cain and Abel, day in and day out.

But what if it *did* produce a baby? A throat-baby? She had never thought of that possibility, and there was good reason. The wisdom of the Fruit assured her that this was not biologically possible. So, I'm not sure why I just brought that up.

Anyway, she finished, spitting in the chamber pot like usual. She should clean that out someday. As he turned back around, she noticed a spot on his left inner thigh. A patch of dry skin, only a few centimeters across, resembling tree bark. She pulled it off without mercy.

"Yikes!" he shouted.

"Sorry," she said, and noticed that he was not bleeding. The light that the moon gave off coming through their cave window was enough to show that this fluid oozing out was not the dark, red fluid of normal blood. It had no color at all; it just glistened in the moonlight.

Maybe this is more of his man stuff, she thought, and lapped it up. No, it was not man stuff. It had a thicker, more sticky consistency, almost like glue, and had a faintly sweet taste to it. It reminded her of what the trees leaked occasionally.

"What was that?" Asked Eve.

"What was what?" he asked.

"That patch on your leg resembling tree bark."

"I don't know," he said. "I had the same thing on my shoulder the other day."

"I've never seen it before," she said, and he

gave her a look. "What?" she asked.

"You have one too," he said.

"What? Where?"

He scraped a finger across her back in answer. She sat, petrified.

"What the... how did it get there?"

"I don't know," he answered. "You mean you hadn't noticed it?"

"No, I can't say I have. Well, don't just lie there, pull it off."

She read worry in his face. "What?" she asked.

"I um, don't think I can. It's taking up your entire back, almost."

"What?" she asked again.

"Yeah. It's huge."

"Where's it coming from?" she asked.

"No idea. Do you think it's an allergic reaction?"

"What does that mean?" asked Eve.

"I don't know. I thought you may know."

"Anyway, can I tell you about my dream now?"

"Absolutely, dear," Adam said, suddenly fully awake. She still had a couple minutes before the Sleep of Adam took over, so she had to make it quick.

"I dreamed that Cain was drinking Abel's

blood."

"Okay," he said.

"What do you think it means?" she asked.

"I think it means that Cain is a lunatic. That's nothing new. Dream explained. Case closed. Anything else I can help you with?"

"I don't know. I'm worried about them, Adam. I think something bad is going to happen."

"Like what? Cain killing Abel? Let's be honest, honey. Abel isn't the brightest bulb in the garden. If Cain kills him, it's survival of the fittest."

"Blasphemous Darwinist crap!"

"I'm just saying, is all."

Eve started to cry, and Adam put his arm under her and held her. "There, there," he said. "Look, if you're that worried about Abel, we'll keep them separated, okay? They can each have their own house far away from each other. That way nothing bad will happen."

"You promise?" she asked.

"Promise. I'll help build them both new huts tomorrow, first thing."

And so, Eve, thus relieved of her anxiety, drifted back to sleep, not dreaming anymore about her two sons. Instead, she thought about the thing on her back just before she crossed over, and she dreamed a dream of becoming a giant tree.

She woke up, paralyzed, thinking she had turned into a tree in her sleep. Gradually, the feeling came back into her limbs, and she could again speak.

"Adam?" she said.

"Blrgr," he answered.

"No, not again. I figured it out. I know what's causing the reactions with our skin. It's the Knowledge Fruits. Don't you see? This didn't happen until we started eating them. This is God's punishment for us."

"Ugh, Eve," he sleepily said, "God already punished us by banishing us to this awful place. That was it. The tree bark growing off of our skins and the twigs poking out from or pores is just a coincidence."

"Are you sure?" asked Eve.

"Positive. Now, go back to sleep."

17. A Talk with the Boys

he next day, Adam sat his two boys down on the couch.

"Ow! Quit it!" Abel shouted.

"Knock it off, Cain," Adam scolded.

"What is it, Dad? I'm awful busy," said Cain.

"Well, I've been doing some thinking. Seems you two boys can't get along. No matter how hard we try to get you to behave, it just keeps getting worse. I think it's time you both got jobs."

Groans from both of the boys.

"Aww."

"But Dad..."

"But Dad nothing. Your mother and I can't continue to live this way, listening to you fight all the time. Plus, we really need help around here. The crops are dying, and the animals are too. They all need tending to. Two people can only do so much. It's high time you chipped in."

"What do you want us to do, Dad?" Abel asked.

"Glad you asked. Abel, since you seem to have a way with animals, I will train you how to be a shepherd."

"Cool."

"I thought you'd like that. As for you, Cain, I want you as far away from Abel as possible. You'll go down to the fields and be a husbandman."

"Haha!" Abel laughed. "Dad wants you to knock up the livestock."

Cain shook his head. "That's not a husbandman, you buffoon. A husbandman tills the soil. Which sounds like the complete opposite of something I want to do, Dad."

"Well, that's just a case of too bad, so sad, love Dad," Adam said. "We all have to do things we don't wanna do around here. Now, the ground may be horrible, but I think we can grow better produce if we tended the ground a little more. "

"Boring," said Cain.

"Now," said Adam, ignoring his son's

comment, "let's get building you guys your own places to live."

"What?" both boys said at once, for different reasons.

"Sweet!" said Cain. "I'll finally get my own pad!"

"Do I have to move out, Daddy?" Abel asked.

"You're both going miles away to do your jobs. It will not be an easy commute to go back and forth every day, especially since the wheel doesn't exist yet. You must stay at your respective farms and only come back once a week with deliveries. Plus, we can't have you both living under the same roof. You'll kill each other."

Cain smirked, as though he had plans to do just that.

"Sounds like you want us to do all the work, Dad," Cain said. "What are you gonna do?"

"Never mind what I'm gonna do. I have a lot of stuff at home I have to take care of. I have to think of a way to get us back to Paradise, which means I have more penance to do. I have to take care of your mother. You don't even want to know about. She wants sixty more children. Although I can't for the life of me even fathom the storm that will bring, she insists that it's the only way to save humanity. I've tried arguing that it's probably not worth saving, but she insists. I argued that that meant you boys would have to reproduce with your own sisters, and she explained that incest is not a sin, and there would be no complications as there are no mutant genes yet. I have a feeling she's been eating a lot more Forbidden Fruit than I have. Anyway, let's get you guys set up."

The boys walked in front of their dad. "Haha," Cain said. "You will need to have sex. With your own sister.

"At least I don't have to have sex with farm animals," Abel said.

"For the last time, that's not what a husbandman does!"

18. Trees

 couple weeks went by, and Cain killed Abel. I mean, hey. Let's face it. We all saw that coming. In fact, Adam was wondering what took him so long. Although he wished it was the other way around, Adam wasn't that overly upset about it. Eve, however, cried every day for the next nine months.

Until their next child Seth was born, which set off a cavalcade. Soon the children started pouring out of Eve like water out of a faucet. Sixty children they had in all. Not possible, you say? Impossible, others who know their prefixes, say? Maybe for those with today's life spans. But when you take into account the fact that they lived for hundreds upon hundreds of years, it was a wonder all they had was sixty. They had stopped eating the Fruit of Knowledge, which not only stopped them from gaining any more intelligence, it also caused them to forget most of the stuff they had learned. One thing they remembered, which was perhaps the most important thing, was that the Fruit was turning them into trees. After years of not touching anything from the Trees, they noticed that no more twigs were growing out in random spots on their bodies, and their skin was taking back the normal consistency and glow of human skin, rather than bark.

"It sure is nice to not have to worry about turning into trees," Adam said.

Soon, however, despite their best efforts, the crops began to die. All except one: The Knowledge Trees were in full bloom all the time.

"Well," Adam said, "we may be out of cucumbers and summer squash, but at least we have meat."

"Baaa!" He heard the sheep scream and ran full tilt to the pens. One by one, they were dropping dead of massive coronaries.

"Hurry!" Adam shouted to Eve. "Grab some salt and some dry rub. We have to get these sheep butchered, dehydrated, and seasoned before the meat goes bad!" Immediately, the

animal flesh started decaying right in front of
their eyes and turned black, setting off a stink
the likes of which they had never smelled. It
was absolutely horrible and made them
retch.

Adam turned to Phil Collins. "Sorry old
buddy," he said. "You're the sacrifice. For the
greater good."

Phil shook his head rapidly.

"Look at it this way, pal. You'll go down in
history as a martyr. That's, like, the ultimate
for a goat, isn't it?"

"Gimme just one more night," Phil Collins
said.

"Sorry, Phil. We love you, but you gotta go.
Daddy's getting hungry."

The goat bolted, never seen again. In case
you're curious, he lived a very long, happy,
and healthy life. He found his way back to
Eden, moved into a luxury condo, met a lady
goat, and started a family of his own. Generation after generation of talking goats later
would spawn one of the most famous goats
ever known, named Biddy, but that's a story
for another time.

"Well, Eve. Looks like it's just you and me
and a Knowledge Tree. What do we do now?"

"The only thing we can do," Eve said. "Let's

dig in. I'm starving."

They both plucked a Fruit from the Tree.

"Let's do this together," Eve said. "On the count of three. Ready? One, two, three." And they both took a bite of their Fruits at the same time.

"You know," Adam said. "This is much better than I remembered."

"Yes," said Eve. "Much sweeter."

They both finished their Fruits and soon grabbed another. They plowed through those, and then on to the next. And the next, and the next. And like salt water only making you thirstier, the Fruits made them hungrier, and that they were gaining more knowledge. More than their human brains could handle. Some were things they had always wanted to know the answers to, and some things they felt they were better off not knowing. But they couldn't stop; they kept eating and eating. Their skin gradually turned to bark, and they paused every now and then to flick the random termite off of each other. After two days of constantly eating, they had consumed every Fruit on the Tree.

"Now what?" asked Eve. "I'm still hungry."

"Me too, daddy," said Luluwa. The kids! He'd forgotten about the kids. After days of no food, they must have been starving.

"Oh, sweetie. You must be so hungry."

"Yes. We'll eat other if we can't find something soon."

As if those words were a trigger, Fruits once again sprang forth from the Trees.

"Quickly," said Adam, "go forth and gather up your brothers and sisters and sons and daughters and nieces and nephews. Tell them there is plenty of Fruit to eat. We shall all become trees together."

"We shall all become what, Daddy?" asked Luluwa.

"Oh, nothing. Hurry now, before your mother and I finish all the Fruit on the Trees.

A few hours later, all children gathered around, and sat noshing on the Fruits. Bark grew on Luluwa, and all their other children, and their children's children too. Roots grew from their toes and sunk deep into the ground. Adam grabbed Eve's hand. They quickly became frozen together.

"Daddy, what's happening?" Aklia asked, which set all the other children to asking their own questions, until their mouths became wooden and could not manage speech.

Adam tried to answer them, but alas, his

mouth was frozen open, too.

A large forest stood where the children used to be.

The sky opened up, and the face of God appeared.

Why, God? Asked Adam in his mind. You owe me...no; You owe all of us, an explanation.

MYSTERIOUS WAYS? God responded.

That will not cut it. I have a feeling this was all a setup. Why did You do this? Why did You make Knowledge Fruit the only food available so we all became trees?

CURIOUS WAYS? Said God, and if Adam could have given him a stern look, he would have.

OKAY, OKAY. YOU ALL BECAME KNOWLEDGE TREES SO THAT FUTURE GENERATIONS MAY EAT FROM YOUR BRANCHES, AND THEY MAY ALSO GATHER KNOWLEDGE, AND THEY TOO MAY BECOME TREES, SO THAT MORE GENERATIONS MAY DO THE SAME. I HAVE BEEN DOING THIS FOR MILLENNIA.

Say what?

YOU REALLY THINK YOU AND EVE WERE THE FIRST ONES TO INHABIT

THE EARTH? HA. THERE WERE SO
MANY BEFORE YOU. ALL THOSE
KNOWLEDGE TREES, THEY WERE ALSO
AT ONE TIME PEOPLE, JUST LIKE YOU.
ISN'T THAT RIGHT, EUGENE? He asked a
tree. HAHA, JUST KIDDING. I KNOW
YOU CAN'T SPEAK. I LOVE PLAYING
LITTLE GAMES LIKE THAT. KEEPS ME
ENTERTAINED.

I still don't see the point, Adam said.

BECAUSE KNOWLEDGE IS A POWER-
FUL THING. BUT EVEN MORE POWER-
FUL IS WEALTH. DO YOU KNOW HOW
MUCH MONEY KNOWLEDGE TREE
WOOD IS WORTH UP HERE? AND
YOU WOULDN'T BELIEVE THE LOVELY
FURNITURE THAT CAN BE MADE FROM
THOSE LIKE YOURSELF. I'LL
TELL YOU, YOU SHOULD BE PROUD TO
BE A TREE.

Seems like a lengthy process to make a
buck or two.

OH, God chuckled, I GOT TIME.

And so, dear reader, if you ever find yourself lost in the forest, and happen upon two
old, wise looking trees that look like their
branches are entwined, that just may be Adam

and Eve, holding hands

I hope you enjoyed A is for Adam as much as Adam did.

Check out an excerpt from my next one, B is for Bear. I promise you a good chuckle.

The lights beaming off the disco ball played tricks with the eye as they danced through Jimmy DiFreno's chest hair. He was quite proud of his chest hair. It was part of his culture to be proud of his chest hair.

He wasn't much to look at. He didn't have the classic chiseled looks of a Rudy Valentino or an Antonio Sabato Jr. You know, looks that could make the ladies swoon while simultaneously being a silent killer. No, he had the stereotypical looks of a James Gandolfini: Six-foot-two, two hundred seventy-five pounds, give or take. He knew that if he kept eating the way he did, he would most likely end up like the late great Gandolfini, but boy, did he love his *gabagool*. And spaghetti and meatballs. And *pasta fazool*. And pie. You get the picture. Not that he wasn't a good-looking guy in his own way; it was just hard to get people to believe that he wasn't in the mob with his appearance being the way it was. I mean, he *was* in the mob, in fact, he was the Don; I'm just saying he couldn't hide the fact.

He usually dressed up very nicely in Armani suits, but when it came time to leave the cozy confines of his office in the back and get down on the dance floor of his own night club, Stella, he donned a pair of jeans and a button-down shirt, unbuttoned halfway, so that his marvelous chest hair could rustle like dried leaves in the wind. He also wore a gold chain, which further accented said chest hair and Italian heritage.

He was at Stella practically every day; however, he only got out on the dance floor a couple nights a week. He usually spent most of his time in the back room, doing books, or other some other business. Most of which was not exactly on the up and up. Stella was a front for a more lucrative, and less tax-collectible, business. Obviously. Every decent mafia crew had several legitimate businesses: laundromats, restaurants, night clubs, assassins-for-hire, birthday clowns, and on and on. A mob without a front to hide behind was like a freight train carrying a cargo of drugs and running over a beautiful Mexican woman who looked an awful lot like Salma Hayek.

Not sure what that means? Jimmy did.

He often got mistaken for a bear. No, not a real bear, since that would be weird to have a real bear in a club. Keep up, dummies. Since he was hairy, and large, and (some may even say) cuddly, occasionally other men would hit on him. He had an ironic vibe about him that most of the overly macho men of the bear persuasion were guilty of affecting. Like Freddie Mercury or Rob Halford, that kind of thing. It didn't happen too often, since this wasn't a gay club. But it happened often enough. And when it did, he would put on airs like it offended him. In reality, though, he felt honored. Not that he'd ever have sex with them; he didn't swing that way. Unless it came to Joe.

Most everyone in the mafia, and especially the Dons, had a little *goomah* on the side. A Don without a *goomah* was like a bald man picking up spare change. So, that's why it came as a shock to Jimmy that his wife Charlene had no clue. There was a possibility that she knew and just chose to never bring it up, but he highly doubted it. Charlene's father was Don Figarazzi. The Don of the very famous Figarazzi family. The funny thing was, his name was also Don.

Anyway, when he got to the age that he was "too old for this crap", he handed the reigns to Jimmy. Sadly, he had no sons of his own, and since Charlene was the apple of Don's eye, it was his decision to give Jimmy the job. That way, his grandson could continue when he was old enough. This pissed off a lot of actual family members, including his brother Don, his nephew Donald, and his three cousins, Don, Don, and Timmy, but Don's decision was Don's decision, and so it stood.

Jimmy's father-in-law knew that he had a *goomah* on the side; it didn't really bother him. It wasn't Don's wrath that concerned him. It was Charlene's. If she found out, not only would she cut his balls off, but she would also convince her father to have him taken out. Even though Jimmy was Don, Don was still the Don of the Don, and there were plenty of actual Figarazzi's that would have been more than happy to do the job.

Don Figarazzi would have killed him if he knew just who Jimmy was fooling around on Charlene with: His best buddy Joe. The Mafia community frowns upon homosexuality. It's a sign of weakness. In Italian dialect they call it a *fanook*, and Jimmy most definitely wasn't one. Now Joe, he wasn't so sure about, but really, who was he to cast aspersions? Joe was his capo, his best friend, and sometimes, his lover. That didn't make him gay, right?

Right?

You see, Joe saved Jimmy's ass in 'Nam. Joe nursed his dog to health when he didn't have a paw to stand on. Joe gave him a place to stay when he got out of the army and had no place to go. Joe rescued his mother from a burning building. He and Joe opened their first hot dog stand together, back when they were just kiddies in Brooklyn. Joe tipped him off on some winning lottery numbers. Joe gave him grape soda when he needed a fine carbonated beverage. All this you may already know; I'm not sure how much Jimmy has divulged to you. And tonight, he got himself a nice hummer in the bathroom. Not the truck, although he had one of those as well. And that would not fit in the bathroom. By hummer, I meant he got his dick sucked by Joe. Oh? I didn't have to explain that? You understood that already by the context? My bad.

Anyway, enough about Joe for now. The evening at Stella was at full swing, but Jimmy had his fair share of paperwork to do before he went home.

.

Mailing list

Want to read more? Don't stop here, the action is just beginning.

Go to www.marcrichardauthor.com and sign up to the mailing list to get lots of cool stuff not available elsewhere.

Please don't forget to post a review. They mean everything to a starving artist. Thank you!

Printed in Great Britain
by Amazon